The Night Before Christmas, Deep Under the Sea

by
Kathie Kelleher

illustrated by
Dan Andreasen

Holiday House / New York

Text copyright © 2012 by Kathie Kelleher
Illustrations copyright © 2012 by Dan Andreasen
All Rights Reserved
HOLIDAY HOUSE is registered in the U.S. Patent and Trademark Office.
Printed and Bound in March 2012 at Kwong Fat Offset Printing Co., Ltd.,
Dongguan City, China.
The text typeface is Steam.
The artwork was created using a combination of digital underpainting
and textures along with traditional oil painting.
www.holidayhouse.com
First Edition
1 3 5 7 9 10 8 6 4 2

Library of Congress Cataloging-in-Publication Data
Kelleher, Kathie.
The night before Christmas, deep under the sea / by Kathie Kelleher; illustrated by Dan Andreasen.
p. cm.
ISBN 978-0-8234-2336-1 (hardcover)
I. Andreasen, Dan, ill. II. Title.
PS3611.E4N54 2011
811'.6—dc23
2011037067

For Mom and Dad,
the two best presents
I ever received
— K. K.

For Katrina
— D. A.

On the night before Christmas, deep under the sea
Marine life was waiting with expectant glee.

Our seashells were hung on the coral with love
In hopes that dear Santa would appear from above.
Young mermaids curled up in their pale oyster beds,
While visions of periwinkles swam through their heads.

I hopped into the kelp
with a rousing leap
And counted bright jingle shells
to lull me to sleep,
When from sea foam above
came a sudden commotion.
Startled out of my bed, I felt
the swell of the ocean.

Up to the porthole I swam like a shark;
I tore back the seaweed then peered through the dark.
The moon shells they glimmered like pearls from the glow
Of luminescent jellyfish gliding below.

Then suddenly diving through briny waves' courses
Came a huge conch shell sleigh and eight lively sea horses.
With a sprightly, tusked driver, it gave me some pause,
Then I knew he quite surely was dear Santa Claus.

Faster than dolphins his aqua team came,
As he gestured and motioned and shouted each name:
"Now, *Dipper*! Now, *Digger*!
Now, *Limpet* and *Quahog*!
On, *Urchin*! On, *Snail*!
On, *Chiton* and *Sea Dog*!

Through the top of the current!
Through the force of the squall!
Now swim away! Swim away! Swim away all!"

As an island lighthouse guides ships safely by
For goodness and glory through storms or bright skies,
So too from the topmast the sea horses drew
With the sleigh full of gifts and Santa Claus too!

Then in an instant
 I heard a sound hail,
The bouncing and swishing
 of each curly tail.
As I pulled back my claw and
 leaned into the sash,
Down through the poop deck
 Santa came with a splash.

Decked out in red rubber from his toes to his collar,
He filled each of our stockings with crisp new sand dollars.
With a bag full of goodies slung over that suit,
He looked like a pirate come hauling his loot.

His eyes, how they sparkled! His tusks,
   how they curled!
His cheeks were bulbous; his nostrils
   were swirled!
His mustachioed mouth held a smile of delight,
And those wiggly whiskers were all wavy
   and white.

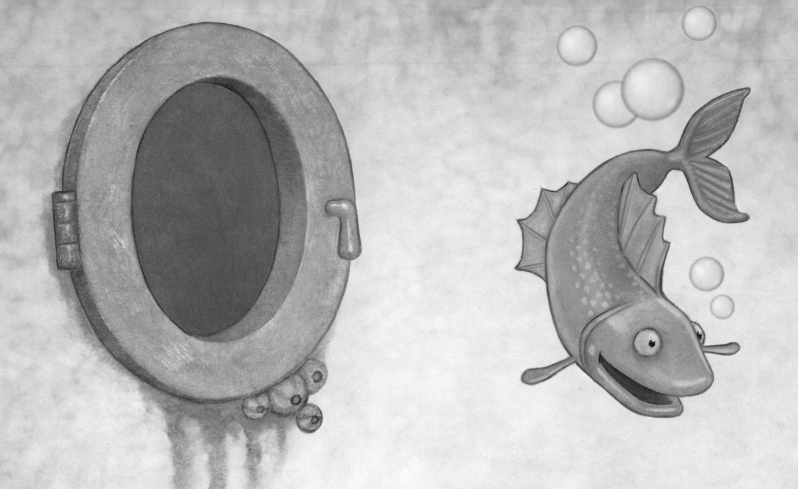

The stem of his pipe rested under his tongue,
And over his head glassy sea bubbles hung.
He had a kind face and a large rotund belly
That bounced as he laughed like a jiggling crown jelly.

Bewitched as I was by this jolly old guy,
Still I cautiously watched from
    my kelp bed nearby.
But a gleam in his eye and a nod of his head
Put my fears to rest without words being said.

He placed polar sea stars on top of our trees
And then turned one hundred and eighty degrees.
Sliding his glasses to the end of his nose,
With a flap of one flipper up the current he rose!

He soon reached his sleigh and to his crew gave a sign,
And away they all swam up that soaring incline.
As the flotilla ascended, he bellowed quite clearly,

"Merry Christmas, my friends!
I love you all dearly!"